TEST OF CHARACTER

JT BALDWIN

"Character is revealed not in moments of crisis, but in the quiet choices made when no one is watching. Do we serve the institution, or do we serve the principles the institution was meant to protect? History will judge us not by our intentions, but by our actions in the moments that mattered most."

— Final journal entry, Chief Minister Pence Garda, dated three days before his resignation

Series Guide | THE PALISADE JOURNALS

RECOMMENDED READING ORDER:

CHRONOLOGICAL TIMELINE:

• 2173 | *I, Marked*
  A girl named Anne becomes a weapon called Snips.

• 2178 | *The Thermecine Road*
  Regal Eldain begins his descent down the road of vengeance.

▶ **2183 | *Test of Character* ◀ You Are Here**
  Victoria Colwell witnesses an unspeakable transfer of power.

• 2189 | *The Broker's Gambit*
  Silver tongued Rhowan Cade gets invited to the Big Leagues.

• 2191 | *Chief Minister*
  The highest office is not enough for Shori Ashford.

PART ONE

The Morning Express

Mid-Spring, 2183 | 0500 | Victoria's Apartment
Government Residential District, CAD Hamilton

Victoria Colwell woke in the pre-dawn darkness and reached instinctively for the familiar weight of her timepiece on the nightstand. The worn bronze felt cool against her palm, a comfort that had become as reliable as her internal chronometer, the natural timekeeping ability calibrated through eight years of service to Chief Minister Pence Garda.

She held the pocket watch for a moment, thumb tracing the smooth crystal face, before setting it carefully back in place. Five o'clock, precisely. No alarm clock required, though the Continental Authority had thoughtfully provided one with all the reliability of a ministerial promise.

She rose from her narrow bed and moved through her morning routine with methodical precision. Twenty minutes for personal preparation, ten minutes for breakfast, and precisely sixty minutes for document review, the sort of disciplined schedule that prevented Chief Ministers from inadvertently declaring war on their own territories.

Her apartment reflected the same elegant restraint: clean lines, quality furnishings selected for durability rather than fashion, everything positioned with deliberate care. The only concession to sentiment was a small framed photograph of weathered Gothic towers rising from an ancient harbor, limestone spires of Keth's oldest college, where serious minds had been shaped for six centuries before the Continental Authority had even existed.

How wonderfully romantic, Victoria reflected, settling at her kitchen table with coffee and the morning's correspondence. *Pining for academic distinction while managing the enthusiastic incompetence that passes for governance in these provincial territories.*

The overnight reports told their familiar story of bureaucratic ambition colliding with arithmetic's inconvenient limitations. Three budget modification requests, each more optimistic than mathematics would support. A grain shipment dispute elevated to ministerial attention, as if trade disagreements required constitutional consideration. And seventeen matters marked "urgent" that would prove neither urgent nor particularly important once subjected to proper analysis.

One does so appreciate the creative interpretation of priority that characterizes frontier administration, Victoria mused, her pen slicing across the summary sheet. *Though I suppose when one's civil service training emphasizes enthusiasm over competence, such confusion becomes inevitable.*

But it was the routine maintenance notification from Fort Delvaine that made her pause. She read the entry twice.

"Routine infrastructure maintenance scheduled during assessment period. Standard safety protocols in effect."

In eight years of managing Pence's correspondence, she had never encountered fortress maintenance during training cycles. Such work invariably occurred between assessments, when facilities stood empty. The timing suggested either remarkable inefficiency or something more deliberately orchestrated.

Curious, she thought, making careful notation. *Though given the Continental Authority's apparent belief that administrative procedure should yield to convenience rather than logic, perhaps I shouldn't be surprised.*

Six-twelve. Perfectly adequate margin for the day's requirements.

⟡

0640 | Chief Minister's Residence

"Good morning, sir." Victoria placed his coffee at the optimal position and opened her briefing folder with practiced efficiency. "I trust the evening concluded satisfactorily?"

Minister Ashford had joined them for what Pence fondly called "family dinner," his way of including promising protégés in informal discussions where real political wisdom was shared rather than the performative nonsense that characterized most official gatherings.

"Quite well, thank you." Pence removed his glasses and focused on her with attention that had sustained him through seven decades of political complexity. "Though I suspect your expression suggests this morning has already provided its customary complications."

"Nothing beyond the usual continental enthusiasm for dramatic timing, sir." Victoria consulted her notes. "Though I should mention that Minister Ashford has confirmed her attendance at today's ceremony. She'll meet us at the fortress."

"Excellent news. Shori has taken such personal interest in Jaden's development over the years." Pence's satisfaction was evident. "Having her witness this milestone means a great deal to both of us."

Victoria felt genuine warmth at his words, though she had to admire how completely Shori had committed to Jaden's development, despite her demanding portfolio.

"Any pressing matters requiring attention before departure?"

Victoria flipped through her correspondence. "The Valorian delegation has encountered the usual complications involving protocol and expectations. Minister Harwick continues his thoughtful consideration of infrastructure proposals, presumably he'll reach a conclusion before the infrastructure requires replacement. And the Calinoka development consortium maintains their optimistic pursuit of radioactive real estate ventures."

"Ah, our persistent friends from Calinoka." Pence's amusement was obvious. "Still convinced that sufficient financial incentive can overcome minor inconveniences like environmental contamination?"

"They've increased their proposed revenue sharing to thirty-five percent, sir. Apparently, they believe enhanced compensation makes residential development compatible with long-term health concerns."

"Their dedication to creative problem-solving is truly remarkable. Though I suspect their definition of 'problem-solving' differs somewhat from conventional approaches to mathematics and mortality."

"Indeed, sir. Their enthusiasm exceeds their grasp of practical limitations by roughly the same margin that separates optimism from systematic delusion."

Pence chuckled. "What time do we depart?"

"The morning express leaves CAD Hamilton at seven-thirty, sir. I've arranged our private compartment and confirmed that no members of the press have managed to secure passage through either competence or corruption."

"Perfect timing as always, Victoria. Your precision continues to amaze me."

0730 | CAD Hamilton Central Station

The morning express to Fort Delvaine represented Continental Authority engineering at its pinnacle: gleaming steel carriages, clockwork scheduling, and sufficient comfort to transport senior officials without subjecting them to commercial travel's indignities. Victoria appreciated the craftsmanship even as she dreaded the necessity, motion sickness being hardly compatible with analytical thinking.

The station buzzed with controlled chaos, steam hissing from locomotives while porters navigated through crowds with practiced efficiency. Salt air drifted in from the nearby harbor, mixing with coal smoke and sweet citrus from vendor carts.

Today's crisis appeared in the form of Harrison, the diplomatic aide who possessed exactly the kind of earnest competence that made Victoria simultaneously protective and mildly exasperated.

"Ms. Colwell, thank heaven you're here." Harrison approached with obvious relief. "We have a developing situation with the Valorian delegation."

"What sort of situation, Harrison?" Victoria accepted the folder while signaling the porter to manage their luggage. "Protocol violations, security concerns, or merely the usual diplomatic enthusiasm for impossible demands?"

"All three, I'm afraid." Harrison's expression suggested he'd been wrestling with this crisis since dawn. "They arrived early, their passenger manifest doesn't match security clearances, and Ambassador Reeves is demanding shipping corridor access that wasn't in the original talks."

Victoria scanned the situation report. "Harrison, the Valorian delegation's early arrival demonstrates commitment to productive negotiations rather than mere protocol observation. Their manifest adjustments reflect natural evolution of diplomatic priorities during travel. One can hardly expect foreign negotiators to maintain rigid adherence to paperwork when circumstances require flexibility."

She handed him a revised protocol schedule addressing each crisis through reframing rather than direct confrontation. "Ambassador Reeves's concerns about shipping access represent legitimate commercial interests that can be addressed through collaborative discussion rather than adversarial positioning. Execute these modifications, report any complications immediately, and remember that today's ceremony reflects the Continental Authority's excellence rather than its occasional tendency toward administrative confusion."

Harrison accepted the folder with evident gratitude and departed. Victoria watched him leave with satisfaction.

"Impressive work," Pence observed from the train car entrance. "Though I suspect 'collaborative discussion' might prove optimistic regarding Ambassador Reeves's current temperament."

"Optimism, sir, is merely analytical precision applied to diplomatic possibilities." Victoria followed him toward their compartment, then paused as a familiar figure approached across the platform.

"Chief Minister Garda, Ms. Colwell." Minister Shori Ashford moved with practiced grace, the transformation from eager young politician into genuine capability evident in every gesture. "What a wonderful surprise. I wasn't expecting to encounter you until we reached the fortress."

"Minister Ashford," Victoria replied with professional courtesy. "What timing. I was just telling the Chief Minister about the Valorian situation."

"Oh yes, the shipping corridor dispute." Shori's smile carried warmth, though her eyes briefly catalogued the platform's security arrangements with systematic attention. "I'm sure you've handled it with your usual efficiency."

Something about the phrasing landed wrong. "Actually, I've reframed the entire negotiation structure to address underlying commercial concerns rather than treating symptoms of deeper policy disagreements."

"How thorough," Shori replied with what might have been mild amusement. "Though sometimes simple solutions work just as well as complex ones."

Simple solutions. As if eight years of crisis management had taught her nothing about the difference between addressing problems and merely postponing them.

"What a distinctive timepiece," Shori said, her attention caught by Victoria's chronometer as she consulted it. "The craftsmanship appears quite exceptional."

Victoria felt pleased by the recognition, though she noted how Shori's observation seemed more analytical than merely polite. "Family piece. Pre-Continental Authority manufacturing."

"How wonderfully authentic. Those older mechanisms were built to endure, weren't they? I imagine the precision must be quite reliable for someone in your position."

"Indeed it is. Some things improve with age rather than requiring constant replacement, a lesson that seems increasingly relevant in contemporary governance."

Before the conversation could continue, the train's departure whistle provided convenient interruption.

"Shall we?" Pence gestured toward their compartment with obvious anticipation.

✵

0850 | Northbound Rail to Fort Delvaine
— ❖ —

The private compartment provided adequate comfort for the two-hour journey, though Victoria would have preferred any mode of transport that didn't involve several tons of metal hurtling across countryside at velocities that challenged both physics and good sense. She settled into her seat with resigned dignity and opened her briefing materials.

Through the windows, the landscape rolled past in shades of spring green, farmland giving way to forests, small towns connected by roads that curved around natural obstacles rather than imposing geometric precision through them.

Pence moved restlessly around the compartment while Victoria reviewed the day's remaining business. Timber allocation proposals that would generate the usual arguments about sustainability versus revenue. Infrastructure funding requests that required more optimism than engineering. The standard fare of territorial governance.

"What about those persistent offshore fishing expansion proposals?" Pence asked, settling into his seat with an expression that carried more weight than routine policy discussion warranted.

"Minister Dacian's office has submitted revised environmental impact assessments for expanded deep-water fishing operations along the northern coast. They maintain that new techniques can increase harvest yields while protecting ecosystem stability, though Minister Ashford's office has been expediting the economic projections."

"And the environmental review conclusions?"

"Mixed findings, sir. The techniques show promise, but marine biologists express concern about impacts on breeding populations. Particularly the bottom-dwelling varieties that serve as foundation elements in the coastal food chain."

Pence was quiet for a moment. "Some ecosystems are more fragile than they appear, Victoria. Once damaged, the effects cascade in ways that aren't immediately obvious to those who measure success in quarterly reports rather than generational stability."

"Indeed, sir. Certain species play roles beyond their apparent significance. Rather like how seemingly minor administrative decisions can have consequences extending far beyond initial projections."

"Precisely." He returned to his seat as the train began its final approach. "Caution serves us well in such matters, particularly when dealing with systems that have proven their stability over time."

The train's rhythm changed as they approached Fort Delvaine, wheels singing against polished steel in a different key. Through the compartment windows, the fortress emerged from rolling hills like mathematics rendered in weathered stone, star-shaped bastions rising from carefully planned approaches.

"How much longer until Fort Delvaine?" Pence asked.

Victoria glanced at her timepiece. "Approximately fifteen minutes, sir. Commander Pa will meet us with appropriate ceremonial arrangements."

"Excellent timing." Pence nodded with satisfaction. "And Jaden's final preparations?"

"All reports indicate exceptional readiness, sir. Cognitive assessments were among the highest recorded, physical training completed successfully, instructors express complete confidence in his capabilities." Victoria felt genuine pleasure delivering positive information about someone who'd become family over the years. "Today should mark a significant achievement for the Garda legacy."

Pence's expression softened with obvious pride. "Four years I've watched him grow at the academy, Victoria. From that grieving boy who'd lost his parents into the exceptional young man completing his studies today. It represents one of my life's greatest satisfactions."

The fortress drew closer, ancient walls rising with impressive solidity. Even at eighty-eight, Pence responded to the sight with visible appreciation, geometric precision of the bastions, morning light catching weathered masonry, flags snapping crisp in the spring breeze.

Victoria watched his anticipation build and felt something twist in her chest. An unexpected tightness that had nothing to do with motion sickness. Fort Delvaine held associations requiring careful mental discipline to navigate, memories she'd spent considerable effort learning to manage.

Five years hadn't been nearly enough time.

Something nagged at her about the battlements as the fortress drew closer. Scaffolding positioned along the northeastern wall. Fresh construction materials visible during what should have been assessment week. The same wall mentioned in this morning's "routine maintenance" notification.

Curious timing for maintenance work. Though I suppose fortress schedules operate on different priorities than administrative convenience would suggest.

But as the train glided to its final stop, Victoria forced herself to focus on the day ahead. Today was about Jaden's future and family celebration. Today was about excellence and the continued Garda legacy.

Nothing more complicated than that.

PART TWO

PERFECT PREPARATION

Mid-Spring, 2183 | 1214 | Rail Station
Fort Delvaine Rail Platform, Delvaine, CA

The train arrived slightly ahead of schedule, wheels singing against polished steel as the massive engine settled into silence with a final exhalation of steam. As the doors opened to the fresh coastal air, Victoria caught the distinctive scent of Fort Delvaine: salt from the Valdris Sea, military polish applied with Germanic thoroughness, and the lingering trace of gunpowder that somehow never quite faded from spaces where power was exercised through precision.

The military platform gleamed with fresh wax, every surface prepared for ministerial inspection. Victoria paused at the compartment doorway, grip tightening on her briefcase as she drew a careful breath.

"Come, Victoria," Pence said gently, his hand resting briefly on her arm. "We have much to be grateful for today."

She stepped onto the platform, immediately cataloging architectural details while setting her briefcase down to attend to more pressing matters. Ancient bastions rising from carefully planned approaches, geometric walls that had defended this territory for centuries, but first, the inevitable media gauntlet.

Victoria smoothed Pence's formal jacket with practiced efficiency, checking that his ceremonial pins were properly aligned and adjusting his collar with the sort of protective attention that had become second nature.

"Eight minutes for questions, sir," she murmured while ensuring his tie sat correctly. "Stick to ceremony significance and Jaden's achievements. Deflect anything about northern development or security protocols."

"Understood." Pence's eyes held a hint of grandfatherly mischief. "Though I suspect these particular vultures are more interested in capturing sentiment than policy disasters."

Victoria stepped forward to address the waiting reporters with diplomatic authority. She fielded questions with precision, redirecting policy inquiries toward ceremonial significance, managing follow-ups with the sort of efficiency that made complex situations appear effortless, before extracting Pence from the media scrum with practiced grace.

"They never give you a break, do they, Chief Minister?" Commander Mikoli Pa approached as Victoria concluded the media obligations, his bearing combining professional courtesy with genuine warmth. "Welcome to Fort Delvaine. It's an honor to host such an important celebration."

"The price of democratic transparency," Pence replied with dry humor. "Though I prefer to think of today as personal investment rather than public obligation."

Victoria shook Pa's hand. Firm. Brief. Precisely what protocol required.

"Commander Pa." Pence's greeting carried genuine pleasure. "The fortress looks magnificent. Your people maintain exceptional standards."

"Thank you, sir. We take considerable pride in preserving both tradition and excellence." Pa turned to Victoria. "Ms. Colwell, I trust the journey wasn't too arduous? The morning express can be challenging for those unaccustomed to extensive rail travel."

"Manageable enough, thank you. Though I'll never understand why the Continental Authority hasn't invested in teleportation research instead of these mechanical death traps."

Pa's chuckle suggested he appreciated her dry humor. "What's your assessment of our defensive positioning?" he asked, noting her continued study of the fortress walls. "I'm curious about a civilian perspective on military architecture."

"Thoughtful integration of historical preservation with modern requirements. The bastions provide excellent overlapping fields of fire while maintaining the fortress's essential character."

"Fields of fire, yes," Pa agreed with mild amusement, "though we'd typically call them 'sectors of observation' for ceremonial purposes."

Victoria felt a slight flush at the gentle correction, out of her element despite her confidence. "Of course. I suppose my administrative experience doesn't extend to proper military terminology."

"Not at all. Your strategic thinking is quite sound."

How refreshingly perceptive, Victoria thought. *Military training apparently cultivates appreciation for efficiency that civilian administration might usefully adopt.*

As they walked through the fortress's geometric pathways, Victoria divided attention between Pa's patient explanations and the steady stream of aides approaching with message slips.

Because apparently, she thought with familiar exasperation, *the Continental Authority would cease to function if I stopped managing administrative emergencies for more than thirty minutes.*

She handled a grain allocation question without breaking stride, sending the nervous young aide away with a solution that would have taken his department three days to reach through proper channels. Pa observed the exchange with evident respect.

"Proper training emphasizes practical application rather than dramatic interpretation, Commander," Victoria said to his unasked question. "Most administrative challenges yield to methodology rather than panic."

1230 | Observation Deck Approach

Footsteps echoed on stone behind them with confident rhythm. Victoria turned to see Minister Shori Ashford catching up, having lingered behind to coordinate with fortress staff.

"Pence," Shori called out, her voice carrying warmth while maintaining exactly the right balance between personal affection and professional respect. "I was hoping I'd catch up before the ceremonies began."

"Walk with me," Pence offered his arm, clearly pleased to share the day's significance.

Shori accepted with practiced grace. Victoria felt genuine appreciation watching their interaction, years of working together creating something beyond professional courtesy into the sort of mentor-student relationship that demonstrated Pence's remarkable ability to nurture potential into capability.

"Difficult to believe it's been four years since you accepted the Coin portfolio," Pence observed as they continued through the fortress pathways.

"Four years this autumn," Shori agreed with fondness that seemed entirely authentic. "Though it feels like yesterday that you first took me under your wing. Has it really been ten years since that first meeting?"

"Ten years since you chose to bring your expertise to civilian governance," Pence said warmly. "The Continental Authority benefited greatly from your years of specialized service."

"It felt like the natural progression. Field work serves its purpose, but policy development offers the chance to create lasting institutional change." A pause. "I'd made some personal decisions that clarified what I actually wanted from public service. Your offer came at exactly the right moment."

"I still remember that budget review when you pulled me aside afterward. 'Politics is chess, not checkers,' you said. 'Every move serves three purposes.'"

Victoria remembered that conversation. She'd been taking notes while Pence dispensed wisdom to his promising protégé.

"Did I actually say that? How remarkably pompous of me." Pence's self-deprecating amusement carried genuine warmth.

"How remarkably wise," Shori corrected with obvious affection. She squeezed his arm gently. "Everything you taught me about strategic thinking has proven invaluable."

"Speaking of strategic thinking," Shori continued, her tone shifting smoothly, "I was hoping we might discuss the infrastructure modernization proposals after today's ceremony. The northern development initiatives."

"Today, Shori?" Pence asked with mild amusement.

"I know the timing isn't ideal. But the Council vote is scheduled for next week, and your insights have always been superior to mine."

Victoria fell into step behind them as Pence began sharing his thoughts on parliamentary strategy, pleased that her schedule had accounted for exactly this sort of impromptu mentoring session.

✿

1245 | Fort Delvaine Observation Deck

—❖—

They reached the observation deck as early afternoon light caught the fortress walls at optimal angles for both ceremonial dignity and practical visibility. The jutting stone platform provided commanding views of the course below, where graduates completed final preparations under Commander Pa's supervision.

"Commander," Pence said, settling into the place of honor, "perhaps you could brief us on what we'll be witnessing today?"

Pa stepped forward with professional pride mixed with ceremonial gravity. "Certainly, sir. We've adapted the fortress's original defensive features for the assessment: climbing sections using the bastion walls, rope work positioned across the old defensive gaps, and tunnel navigation through the underground networks."

Victoria studied the climbing wall. The scaffolding positioned along the northeastern face caught her attention, the same wall mentioned in this morning's maintenance notification.

"Commander," she said, "I noticed the maintenance notification this morning mentioned work scheduled during the assessment period. That's rather unusual timing, isn't it?"

Pa's expression shifted slightly, professional courtesy masking what might have been mild irritation. "Standard infrastructure maintenance, Ms. Colwell. We coordinate with assessment schedules as circumstances allow."

"Of course. Though in eight years of managing ceremonial schedules, I've never encountered fortress maintenance during active training cycles. The timing seems..."

"The timing is perfectly adequate," Shori interjected with a warm smile that somehow managed to sound dismissive. "I'm sure Commander Pa has everything well in hand. Sometimes we administrative types worry too much about details that operational people handle routinely."

Administrative types. As if eight years of crisis management qualified as mere worry rather than professional expertise specifically designed to catch exactly these sorts of irregularities.

"Indeed," Victoria replied, diplomatic courtesy sharpened to a razor's edge. "Operational perspectives occasionally overlook administrative subtleties that prevent larger crises."

Shori's smile remained perfectly pleasant. "Absolutely. Though sometimes the simplest explanation is the correct one."

Sometimes the simplest explanation. Victoria's gaze lingered on the scaffolding along the northeastern bastion. *Curious timing indeed.*

"The climbing wall incorporates masonry from the original 1789 construction," Pa continued, clearly eager to redirect. "We've maintained historical integrity while ensuring contemporary safety standards."

Ancient stone, Victoria thought. *Built to endure, tested by time, proven through centuries of reliable service. Though apparently not immune to convenient maintenance timing.*

Below them, twelve young graduates were systematically removing their formal navy and gold dress jackets, folding them with military precision before conducting final equipment checks in their practical dark field gear. Victoria could identify Jaden among the formation, tall like all Garda men, but with the more delicate features inherited from his mother's side and the distinctive reddish tint to his hair that caught the afternoon light.

"There he is," Pence murmured with unmistakable pride.

Victoria followed his gaze, feeling warmth for the young man who'd become family over the years.

"An exceptional graduate, sir," Pa reported. "His instructors consistently praise his dedication and capability. Cognitive assessments were among the highest we've recorded."

"Intelligent preparation," Shori said with obvious satisfaction. "I'm glad to see he has listened to me and my caution about charging headfirst into the unknown. Proper planning ensures success."

Pa nodded. "Honestly, at this point the physical course is largely ceremonial. The real evaluation happened during their four years of study. Today is about honoring tradition and celebrating completion."

✧

1300 | The Ceremony Begins

— ❖ —

"There," Pa pointed toward the formation's center. "Candidate Oram, third position from the left."

Jaden stood with calm confidence that spoke to months of preparation and natural family temperament. Even from the observation deck, his composed demeanor was apparent. No nervous adjustments. No last-minute equipment verification. No signs of anxiety.

"Standard Garda family temperament," Pence said with obvious pride. "Steady performance under pressure has always characterized our service tradition."

The instructor raised his arm in preparation, then dropped it decisively. The first graduate stepped onto the balance beam, arms extended for stability. The ceremony had officially begun.

Victoria found herself genuinely invested in each graduate's performance despite the steady stream of administrative interruptions requiring her attention. She'd watched Jaden develop from grieving teenager into this confident young man, had been part of countless family dinners where he and Pence discussed military history with intellectual engagement.

This isn't mere professional interest, she acknowledged. *This is personal investment in family success.*

One by one, candidates navigated the initial obstacles with varying degrees of success. The rope section eliminated two candidates, not failures in any absolute sense, but clear indications they required more extensive preparation.

Victoria found herself holding her breath as each candidate attempted the challenges, hands gripping her notepad with intensity that had nothing to do with ceremonial observation.

"Are you at all nervous?" Shori asked quietly.

"Not in the slightest," Pence replied, though his hands had unconsciously gripped the observation rail. "He's been preparing for this assessment his entire life."

Jaden stepped onto the balance beam with unhurried confidence. His movements were economical and precise. No wasted energy. No unnecessary corrections. He completed the beam section with fluid competence, then advanced to rope work with identical steady rhythm.

"Excellent, my boy. Excellent," Pa said softly, unable to hide his pride.

The young man moved across the rope obstacles with apparent ease, hand over hand, maintaining perfect spacing and rhythm. He completed the section efficiently and advanced to tunnel navigation, crawling through narrow passages that threaded between the fortress's original defensive positions.

"Excellent time progression," Pa noted, consulting his pocket timepiece. "Well within acceptable parameters for successful completion."

The tunnel section led to a brief rest position before the assessment's final challenge: the climbing wall built into the northeastern bastion's original stonework. It rose forty feet from the fortress floor to a platform that marked successful completion.

Victoria's gaze locked on the climbing wall. Ancient stone. Centuries old. Tested by countless previous candidates.

Jaden emerged from the tunnel system and paused at the wall's base, studying available hand and footholds with methodical attention. Even from the observation deck, his approach was evident. No rush. No wasted motion. Careful planning before commitment.

The climbing wall offered multiple route options. Jaden selected a middle path that balanced efficiency with security, beginning his ascent with the same steady confidence he'd demonstrated throughout the entire assessment.

Ten feet. Twenty feet. Thirty feet.

"Exceptional climbing technique," Pa said quietly. "Textbook form and execution."

"And Garda physique!" Pence added, leaning forward in his seat.

Victoria felt her heart pounding. Everything proceeding exactly as they'd hoped.

"You should be very proud," Shori said. "He's a credit to everything the Garda family represents."

Thirty-five feet. Nearly at completion.

The tightness in Victoria's chest as she watched Jaden approach the final section. Almost there. Almost finished.

Thirty-eight feet up, Jaden reached for his next handhold with the same confident precision he'd maintained throughout the entire assessment.

He had only two more feet to succeed. Two feet that would complete his assessment and start the next path in his life.

He would never make it.

PART THREE

THE BREAK

Mid-Spring, 2183 | 1347 | Observation Deck
Baldwin Building, UMC | Fort Delvaine, CA

The sound, barely more than a sharp crack in the afternoon air, made Victoria's world stop.

Jaden was thirty-eight feet up the climbing wall when the ancient stone gave way beneath his left hand.

Silence.

Complete, absolute silence stretched across the observation deck like a held breath. Victoria watched Jaden's body tumble through empty air, striking the stone below with a sound that would haunt her forever.

Then Commander Pa lunged for his radio. "Medical! Emergency medical to the climbing wall! We have a man down!"

Chaos erupted. Voices everywhere: shouts, orders, the scrape of chairs. Victoria couldn't move. Couldn't think. Could only stare down at Jaden's motionless form on the stones below.

"Jaden!" Pence's cry tore through everything. Raw, broken anguish. He staggered to the rail, gripping it like it was the only thing keeping him upright.

Voices carried from below, disciplined and urgent:

"...get him stabilized..."

"...structural failure..."

"...coordinate with medical..."

Victoria stood frozen, fragments washing over her without meaning.

Shori was talking to Pence, her hand on his arm. Something about medical staff, about staying with Jaden. The words floated past Victoria like everything else.

Pence aged ten years in ten seconds, his face gray with shock and grief. The strong, dignified leader she'd served for eight years looked suddenly, devastatingly fragile.

Victoria wanted to move, to help, to do something. But she could only stand there, absorbing fragments of a world that had just shattered completely.

1348 | Emergency Transport

The ambulance swayed through curves as it raced toward CAD Hamilton's medical complex, emergency lights painting the interior in alternating red and white. Victoria sat numbly in the corner, still processing fragments of what had happened.

Jaden lay unconscious on the stretcher, his face pale beneath the emergency blankets. Medical personnel worked around him with quiet efficiency, monitoring vital signs and preparing for the hospital handoff.

Pence sat beside the stretcher, holding his grandson's hand with desperate gentleness. His face had aged a decade in the past hour.

"I don't understand," Pence said quietly, his voice breaking. "He was doing so well. Everything was perfect. How could this happen?"

Shori leaned forward with compassionate authority. "These old fortress walls can be unpredictable, Pence. When the left handhold gave way under his weight, there was nothing anyone could have done."

Victoria's mind snapped into sudden focus.

"I'm sorry, Minister Ashford," she said, her voice sharper than intended. "Could you repeat that? How did you know it was the left handhold that failed?"

A flicker of something crossed Shori's expression, there and gone in an instant. She smiled with gentle patience. "Oh, I was just speculating based on what we could observe from the deck. Though of course, we'll need the engineers to determine exactly what happened." She turned back to Pence with renewed sympathy. "These ancient stone walls can fail in any number of ways. The important thing now is getting Jaden the best possible care."

Victoria stared at her, something cold settling in her stomach. From the observation deck, they'd been too far away to see which specific handhold had failed. The detail was too precise, too certain for mere speculation.

But Shori had already moved on, discussing medical facilities and specialist options with comprehensive knowledge that seemed remarkably well-prepared.

Victoria remained silent for the rest of the journey, but her mind was no longer numb. Something was very wrong here.

She just couldn't prove it yet.

✧

1630 | Medical Assessment

— ❖ —

Dr. Kellman finished her examination and turned to face them with the sort of professional gravity that preceded life-changing news. Jaden lay unconscious in the hospital bed, monitors beeping steadily around him.

"The damage is concentrated in the lower thoracic region," she said quietly. "Motor function will return partially, but not to the level required for active military service. With intensive rehabilitation, we expect significant improvement. Mobility assistance will be necessary initially, though many patients eventually transition to walking aids."

The words hung in the sterile air like a death sentence for everything Jaden had worked toward.

"His military career..." Pence began, unable to finish.

"I'm sorry," Dr. Kellman said with genuine compassion. "That path is closed to him now."

Shori moved immediately to Pence's side, her hand resting gently on his shoulder. "Whatever Jaden needs for rehabilitation, whatever adaptive training might help him find new purpose, consider it done. I'll personally ensure he receives every opportunity to rebuild his future."

Victoria watched this display of support, remembering the handhold comment from the ambulance. Something about Shori's immediate, comprehensive response felt too prepared.

"This is terrible timing," Shori continued with appropriate regret. "I know I need to be here for him, and for you, Pence. But I can only postpone my Council duties for so long." She squeezed his shoulder gently. "Victoria is here. I'm sure she'll be invaluable in whatever support is required."

After Shori left, silence settled over the room like a weight.

"Pence," Victoria said carefully, moving closer to his chair. "I need to tell you something. About today... something feels wrong. I can't explain it exactly, but the timing, the way things happened..." She paused, knowing how this would sound. "I don't think this was an accident."

Pence didn't respond immediately, his eyes fixed on Jaden's pale face.

"Did you know," he said suddenly, his voice distant, "Penny had a thing for red coastal lobster? You could only find the good ones up in UAD Port Franklin, couldn't get them anywhere else that was worth a damn. I took Jaden there shortly after his parents' passing. He devoured them, couldn't get enough. Never understood the fondness for it myself, but mother and son both loved them equally."

His voice wavered, memories overtaking present grief.

"She used to laugh at how seriously Jaden took his studies, even as a boy. Said he got that from her father, my analytical mind, she called it. Always looking for patterns, connections..." Pence's hands trembled in his lap. "Vicky... I'm not sure I'm strong enough to do this again."

Victoria felt tears burning her eyes as she watched this strong man break under the weight of losing his family piece by piece. Without a word, she moved to his chair and wrapped her arms around him, not the professional gesture of a devoted aide, but the fierce embrace of someone who understood that some losses cut too deep for words.

Pence leaned into her support, his shoulders shaking with silent grief as the monitors beeped their steady rhythm around Jaden's still form.

They sat in silence, holding onto each other while the afternoon light faded through the hospital windows.

1800 | Hospital Corridor

— ❖ —

Victoria walked the sterile hallway toward the vending machines, needing movement, needing air, needing something other than the weight of grief pressing down on everything.

Her mind raced as she moved, fragments from the day swirling without pattern or connection:

Shori's immediate efficiency. The engineers arriving with exactly the right equipment. "When the left handhold gave way," how could she know that? The maintenance timing she'd questioned. Dismissed concerns. "Administrative types worry too much." Everything proceeding so smoothly, so prepared.

She stopped in front of the vending machine, staring at rows of snacks without seeing them. The inconsistencies buzzed in her head like static, pieces that didn't fit together yet, but felt wrong, felt orchestrated.

Too many coincidences. Too much preparation. Too much knowledge.

Victoria fed coins into the machine and pressed buttons without conscious choice. The mechanism whirred, then released whatever she'd selected with a sharp mechanical thunk as it dropped into the collection bin.

The sound cut through the hospital quiet like a decision being made.

Victoria retrieved her purchase and stood in the fluorescent corridor, understanding that something fundamental had shifted. The grief and shock were still there, but underneath them, something harder was crystallizing.

Someone had done this to Jaden. To Pence. To their family.

And she was going to find out who.

PART FOUR

INTELLIGENCE GATHERING

Mid-Spring, 2183 | Three Days Later, 0800 | Pence's Study
Chief Minister's Residence, CAD Hamilton

Victoria found Chief Minister Pence Garda surrounded by the accumulated chaos of three days' worth of postponed decisions. Papers covered his desk in uncharacteristic disorder, and he sat staring at a letter with the sort of vacant exhaustion that came from grief colliding with governmental responsibility.

"Good morning, sir." Victoria set his coffee at the precise angle he preferred and opened her briefing folder. "I've rescheduled the Infrastructure Committee meeting to accommodate your request for more time with the budget reconciliation reports."

"Change it again. I can't deal with Branok's endless proposals for expanding everything today."

Victoria made a note. "Of course. That's the fourth meeting I've moved this morning."

"Then perhaps you should stop scheduling things I explicitly said I didn't want to attend," Pence snapped, his voice carrying an edge that reminded Victoria of the political fighter who'd held power for decades.

"Sir, with respect, you asked me yesterday to maintain your normal schedule to project stability. The Infrastructure Committee expects your input on the northern development proposals, and Minister Drayce has been asking..."

"I don't give a damn what Drayce is asking!" Pence's political fire flared suddenly. "Half these people are circling like vultures, waiting to see if I'm too broken to fight their pet projects. The other half are pushing through initiatives they know I'd normally block because they think I'm distracted."

He stood abruptly, pacing to the window with movements that showed both his age and his frustration. "Do you think I don't see what's happening? Shori's expediting those fishing expansion reviews. Korvyn's suddenly interested in fortress security protocols. Everyone's got an angle, and they're all betting I'm too devastated to notice."

Relief that his political instincts remained sharp. Concern that he was burning energy he couldn't spare.

"You're absolutely right," Victoria said with quiet firmness. "They are circling. Which is exactly why maintaining your schedule sends the message that you're still fully engaged and capable of blocking whatever schemes they're advancing."

The fight went out of him as suddenly as it had appeared. He slumped back into his chair, looking every one of his eighty-eight years.

"Victoria," he said quietly. "I'm worried that this event is going to have consequences beyond the obvious ones."

She closed her briefing folder and gave him her complete attention.

"I can feel the tide turning. Allies are questioning my judgment. Opponents are using Jaden's accident to suggest our family has been compromised, that I'm emotionally unfit for leadership. Every policy position I've held is suddenly open for renegotiation because they think I'm too weak to defend them."

He rubbed his temples with hands that trembled slightly. "I can't fight them and investigate what's really happening. I don't have the energy for both battles, and I can't trust anyone in the normal channels."

"What do you need me to do?"

"I need you to locate someone for me." Pence opened his desk drawer and withdrew a sealed envelope. "Agent Vanessa Kaine. I encountered her several years ago through professional connections. She has the sort of capabilities that might help us understand what really happened at Fort Delvaine without alerting certain parties to our interest."

Victoria accepted the envelope, recognizing security classifications well above her normal clearance level. "What sort of capabilities, sir?"

"The sort that operate outside normal governmental channels." Pence's precision was careful. "Agent Kaine works independently, but she understands threats that conventional oversight might miss."

"I'll find her, sir."

"Thank you, Victoria." Softly. "I need to know what really happened to my grandson. And I suspect you're the only person I trust enough to find out."

✿

Victoria's Investigation
—— ❖ ——

The secure terminal returned NO RECORD FOUND.

Victoria stared at the screen. In eight years of government service, she'd never encountered someone who simply didn't exist in the system. Everyone had records: personnel files, security clearances, employment history. But Agent Vanessa Kaine appeared to be a ghost.

What kind of person does the Chief Minister know who operates completely outside official channels?

The government archives yielded what the database couldn't. Hours of manual searching through newspaper clippings and police reports produced a single Hamilton Tribune mention from six months prior, buried in a crime report: "Sources indicate that private investigator V. Kaine provided assistance to local authorities in resolving the warehouse district incident."

Private investigator. That explained the lack of government records, but not how Pence knew her or why he trusted her with this.

The article included an address in Hamilton's commercial district. Victoria checked the afternoon train schedule. She could be there by evening.

✦

1800 | Hamilton Commercial District

The address led to a nondescript building wedged between a bookstore and a tea shop. No nameplate, no directory, just a narrow door with a buzzer system. She checked her notes twice before pressing the button marked "3B."

The intercom crackled. "Yeah?"

"I'm looking for Agent Kaine," Victoria said with diplomatic precision. "I have a matter of some urgency to discuss."

Silence. Then: "Third floor. Door's open."

Victoria climbed the narrow stairs, her briefcase in hand and her expectations uncertain. She found the door marked 3B standing slightly ajar and knocked politely.

"Come in," came a voice from inside.

Victoria entered what appeared to be a combination office and workshop. Maps covered one wall, technical equipment she couldn't identify occupied several tables, and the air carried the scent of coffee and something metallic. A woman sat at a desk with her back to the door, working on what looked like surveillance photographs.

"Agent Kaine?" Victoria began with professional courtesy. "My name is Victoria Colwell. I'm here on behalf of Chief Minister Garda regarding a matter of considerable importance that requires your particular expertise."

The woman turned in her chair, studying Victoria with sharp green eyes that cataloged threats with professional thoroughness. Tall. Athletic. Dark hair pulled back severely. An expression that suggested she was accustomed to environments considerably more dangerous than government offices.

"Who the hell are you?"

"Excuse me?" Victoria's diplomatic training kicked in with indignant precision. "I just introduced myself, and properly I might add. Are you or are you not Agent Kaine?"

Nessa leaned back in her chair, studying Victoria like she was some exotic species that had wandered into the wrong habitat. "Depends who's asking and why they think they need to know."

"I've already explained that I'm here on behalf of Chief Minister Garda regarding a matter of considerable..."

"Lady, you showed up at my door spouting titles and talking about 'matters of importance' like you're reading from a government handbook." Nessa's voice carried the sort of casual authority that suggested she was used to cutting through exactly this type of diplomatic nonsense. "That tells me you're either completely new to this kind of work or you think I'm stupid enough to be impressed by official-sounding language."

"I assure you that my credentials and the urgency of this matter..."

"Stop." Nessa held up a hand. "You're obviously educated, probably good at your job, and clearly think that proper procedure will get you what you want. But I can already tell you're going to waste twenty minutes dancing around whatever brought you here."

She stood. "So let's skip the verbal foreplay. Get to the point. Why does Pence want me?"

"I have something from Chief Minister Garda," Victoria said, producing the sealed envelope from her briefcase.

Nessa took it, broke the seal, and read quickly. Something shifted in her expression: surprise, then understanding, then what might have been respect. She folded the letter carefully and tucked it away without comment.

"All right." She settled back into her chair. "Tell me what happened."

"Someone tried to murder his grandson," Victoria said, the diplomatic language finally stripped away.

"Someone attacked Jaden during his military assessment," Victoria continued, diplomatic precision returning now that she had Nessa's interest. "The circumstances surrounding the incident demonstrate a pattern of systematic preparation that suggests..."

"Stop." Nessa's voice cut through her momentum like a blade. "You're doing it again."

"Doing what?"

"Talking like a government report. Someone attacked the kid, you said. That's the important part. Everything else is you trying to sound official instead of just telling me what happened."

"I'm attempting to provide proper context for the events that..."

"Lady, I can already tell you've got about fifteen different things rattling around in that educated head of yours, and you're trying to organize them into some kind of diplomatic presentation. But you're not briefing the Council. You're talking to someone who needs facts, not fancy language."

"Sit down," Nessa continued, gesturing to a chair. "Empty that dense head and focus for five minutes. Tell me what you actually saw, what you actually heard, and what made you think someone tried to kill the kid. Just the facts, no diplomatic interpretation."

Victoria remained standing, her briefcase clutched tight. "I hardly think..."

"That's your problem right there. You're thinking instead of talking. Sit. Down."

For the first time in eight years of managing political crises, Victoria found herself completely outmaneuvered. She sat.

"Good. Now start from the beginning, and if you use the phrase 'systematic preparation' or 'proper context' I'm throwing you out. What happened to the kid?"

Victoria drew a careful breath.

"Jaden fell," she began simply. "But everything about it felt wrong."

She closed her eyes. Felt ridiculous. Recognized that normal approaches weren't working with this woman.

"It's all chaos at first," she said quietly. "Everything happening at once, people shouting, equipment appearing..."

"Block that out," Nessa said firmly. "What did you actually see?"

Victoria pushed through the noise and confusion to find the details that had been nagging at her for three days.

"The transport. Minister Ashford was comforting Pence, explaining what happened. She said... 'When the left handhold gave way under his weight.' But we were too far away to see which handhold failed. I asked her how she knew, and she covered by saying it was speculation."

"Keep going."

"Commander Pa's face when the engineers arrived. Not shock or surprise. Regret. Like he knew something he couldn't say." Her eyes remained closed, the fragments becoming clearer. "The engineers had exactly the right equipment, arrived too quickly. Their explanations sounded rehearsed."

"What else?"

"Her efficiency. She was coordinating response before anyone else even moved. She knew exactly who to call, what needed to happen. It felt prepared."

Victoria opened her eyes to find Nessa studying her with sharp attention. No longer dismissive.

"The maintenance timing I'd questioned that morning. Everyone dismissed my concerns as administrative worry. But the scaffolding was positioned exactly where the stone failed."

Nessa was quiet for a long moment. Then she stood and began gathering equipment from around the office: tools Victoria didn't recognize, a camera, what looked like some kind of measuring device.

"Come on," Nessa said, shouldering a pack.

"Where are we going?"

"Fort Delvaine. Let's get a look at that wall."

Victoria glanced toward the darkening windows. "But it's nearly nine o'clock..."

"You got somewhere else to be?"

Her carefully ordered world of schedules and proper procedures had just been completely upended by someone who operated outside all normal rules.

"No," she said quietly. "I suppose I don't."

PART FIVE

Building the Case

Mid-Spring, 2183 | 0000 | Rail Station
Fort Delvaine, CA

"How exactly do you know your way around..." Victoria began quietly.

"Questions later," Nessa interrupted, leading them up a narrow service stairway. "Evidence first."

They emerged onto the platform at the top of the climbing wall, forty feet above the courtyard where Jaden had fallen three days earlier. Victoria felt her stomach tighten at the proximity to devastation, but forced herself to focus.

Nessa moved to the edge without hesitation and swung herself over the side.

"What in hell are you doing?" Victoria hissed, rushing to the edge as Nessa rappelled down to the broken section with equipment she'd produced from her pack.

"Getting a closer look at your crime scene," Nessa called up softly, playing a small light over the damaged stone. The subtle green glow illuminated details invisible from the observation deck. "Hold on."

Victoria watched in fascination and horror as Nessa examined the break while hanging precariously on the side of the climbing wall with no safety equipment. She extracted a fragment from the damaged handhold, then climbed back up with efficient movements that suggested this sort of thing was routine.

"Here," Nessa said, handing Victoria the stone fragment. "What do you see?"

Victoria held the piece up to catch the moonlight, turning it slowly in her fingers. The break surface showed discoloration, metallic traces that shouldn't exist in natural stone failure.

"Brass residue," she said slowly. "And some kind of corrosion pattern."

"Smell it."

Victoria brought the fragment closer. A sharp, acrid scent that made her face wrinkle in distaste. "Chemical. Acidic."

"Right." Nessa pocketed the evidence with grim satisfaction. "You might be onto something after all, princess. That's thermite residue. Someone used controlled demolition to weaken that handhold."

Victoria stared at the fragment, understanding crystallizing with horrible clarity. "Calculated for maximum vulnerability. They knew exactly when he'd reach for it."

"Engineered failure disguised as ancient stone giving way. Professional work. Expensive work. The kind that requires advance planning and access to specialized materials."

"Who would have that kind of access?"

"Let's go find out." Nessa shouldered her pack. "Time to break some laws. Hope you're ready to become a criminal."

Victoria followed her toward the administrative building. Eight years of perfecting protocols. Eight years of defending institutional procedure. Those things had failed Jaden catastrophically. The truth was somewhere behind a locked door.

For Jaden, for Pence, for justice, she was ready.

✧

0015 | Infiltration
— ❖ —

Nessa led them through the fortress like she'd memorized the blueprints, while Victoria tried not to think about how her comfortable evening of reviewing budget allocations had transformed into committing felonies in military installations.

They crouched behind a stone pillar as footsteps echoed from the main corridor. Nessa held up a hand for silence.

The footsteps faded. Nessa gestured forward.

"Move! Now!" she whispered.

Victoria hurried across the open corridor, her heels clicking against stone despite her efforts at stealth.

"Oh dear," she muttered as Nessa shot her a look that could have frozen the harbor.

"Take those shoes off. They make too much noise."

Victoria stared at her in horror. "You want me to walk barefoot through a military fortress? These stockings cost more than..."

"I want you to not get us shot because you're clattering around like a show horse."

With as much dignity as she could muster, Victoria removed her shoes and held them carefully. The stone floor was cold against her stockings.

"Limestone, actually," Victoria replied to a comment about her education that she refused to dignify with a full response. "Gothic limestone spires, to be exact. Only a privileged few have ever glimpsed the interior halls."

"I can see you ringing bells," Nessa said flatly.

They reached the administrative building in bristling silence. Nessa produced a lockpicking toolkit and worked on the door with efficiency that made Victoria simultaneously grateful and deeply uncomfortable.

"You were serious about the breaking the law part, weren't you?" Victoria asked quietly.

"Aren't you quick? Must be all that expensive education."

"I'll remind you I didn't get my education at the local penitentiary."

The lock clicked open. Nessa pocketed her tools and pushed the door open.

"After you, princess. Try not to trigger any alarms with those superior analytical capabilities."

⚙

0030 | The Office
— ❖ —

Inside, Nessa went straight to the filing cabinets, pulling out folders and spreading them across a desk. Victoria noticed the small television in the corner, its tube screen humming with warm electrical glow.

She switched it on, keeping the volume low.

Chief Minister Ashford was speaking. "Chief Minister Garda has served our continental government with distinction for decades. Recent tragic events have tested his resolve, but his commitment to constitutional principles remains unshakeable."

Victoria's focus sharpened. This was political theater at its finest, but the timing felt orchestrated.

"However," Shori continued, her tone shifting with practiced precision, "recent events have revealed important vulnerabilities in our current oversight mechanisms that require immediate legislative attention."

Enhanced oversight. The phrase landed like a blow. Victoria had written similar words before, calibrated them, polished them, delivered them to ministers. But now they sounded like chains being forged in real time.

"Are you seriously trying to get us caught?" Nessa appeared behind her, clutching procurement documents. "Turn that off before..."

"Sometimes it's better to listen than talk," Victoria said, pointing at the screen.

Shori's performance continued. "I propose the immediate establishment of enhanced oversight committees with specialized investigative authority for identifying and neutralizing threats that traditional mechanisms might overlook."

Victoria looked at Nessa. "I think we may have found our orchestrator."

Nessa stared at the screen. Something shifted behind her eyes. Not surprise. Something darker. Something that carried the weight of years.

"Shori Ashford?" Her voice carried a quality Victoria couldn't identify. Something between recognition and denial. "The Shori Ashford?"

"You know her."

Silence. Nessa's hands stilled on the files she was holding. When she spoke, her voice had dropped to something quieter than Victoria had heard from her.

"Yeah. I know her." A pause that held more than the words around it. "We knew each other. Long ago. Bad end."

Victoria watched her carefully. For the first time, Nessa looked unsure. Eyes flicking from the screen to the files and back. Not a strategist calculating risk. Someone trying to reconcile the person they knew with the evidence in their hands.

"You can't be serious," Victoria said.

"None of that matters." Nessa gathered the scattered files with sudden urgency. "The evidence you need is here."

✿

0045 | The Scope of Betrayal

— ❖ —

She spread procurement documents across the desk. "Kellworth," she said, pointing to signature after signature. "Deputy Aide Martin Kellworth authorized everything. Materials, access, timing."

"Perfect fall guy. Gambling debts, family financial pressures." Victoria studied the paperwork. "Someone recruited him months ago."

"Materials procurement for specialized compounds. Substances that don't appear on normal supply lists. Facility access schedules that coincide exactly with Jaden's assessment timing. Personnel authorizations that put Kellworth on site during the precise window when your boy would be climbing."

She pointed to dates, signatures, authorization codes. "Six months of coordinated preparation. This wasn't some desperate gambler making a quick score. This was professional recruitment and operational coordination."

"Someone with access to classified fortress protocols and detailed knowledge of Jaden's training schedule," Victoria said.

"Someone who knew your family well enough to understand exactly how to maximize psychological devastation."

"She's been like family for years," Victoria said quietly. "Pence trusts her completely. She mentored Jaden, knew his psychology, his methods, his vulnerabilities..."

Nessa's hands stilled on the documents. Something vulnerable flickered across her expression before composure reasserted itself. "Everything."

"Everything." Victoria's voice was barely a whisper. "She had access to everything she needed to destroy him while appearing to be the perfect supportive family friend."

Nessa stared at the evidence. Then she shook her head.

"Look, Shori is driven and a bit of a narcissist... but there's no way she would spend all this time working under Pence and then pull the rug out from underneath him. I mean, that dude is ancient... she could have just waited a few more years and let him..."

"Let him what?" Victoria asked.

Nessa caught herself. "Let him retire gracefully."

"You still care about her," Victoria said quietly.

"I care about the truth." But her voice lacked conviction. "And rushing to conclusions based on circumstantial evidence is exactly how innocent people get destroyed by vengeful institutions."

"Agent Kaine," Victoria said carefully, "I believe we may be in considerably more danger than either of us initially anticipated."

"Yeah." Nessa was still looking at the files as if hoping they might tell a different story. "Probably."

Victoria was about to continue when Nessa froze, her head tilted slightly, listening to something Victoria couldn't hear. In one swift motion, she switched off the television and doused her light.

"Not a sound," Nessa whispered.

The office plunged into darkness. Victoria could hear her own breathing, suddenly too loud, and the rapid beating of her heart. Then, faintly through the walls, the distinctive click-clack of military boots on polished stone.

The footsteps approached. Paused at their door. The distinct rattle of someone testing the handle. Twice. Longer than routine.

Victoria's academic mind, even in terror, couldn't help wondering what military prison would be like for someone whose only previous criminal experience involved overdue library books.

The footsteps moved on. Checking each door with methodical thoroughness.

Nessa waited a full minute before producing her light again.

Victoria's legs were still trembling as they prepared to leave.

"Let's take these," Nessa said quietly, gathering the procurement documents and evidence files. "We have what we need. Time to head back."

⚙

0300 | Return Journey

— ❖ —

The tram ride back to CAD Hamilton swayed gently through the pre-dawn darkness. Victoria succumbed to exhaustion that felt more like emotional crash than physical fatigue.

She dozed fitfully against the window, lulled by the rhythmic sound of wheels on tracks. For now, at least, they were safe and moving toward whatever came next.

When she woke, they'd be back in Hamilton. Back to discovering the truth.

And with luck, not killing each other to find it.

PART SIX

VICTORIA'S GAMBIT

Mid-Spring, 2183 | 0730 | Victoria's Apartment
Government Residential District, CAD Hamilton
— ❖ —

Victoria woke with the same habitual reach for her timepiece. But something felt wrong. The light filtering through her curtains was too bright, too warm for her usual pre-dawn routine.

She'd overslept. Nearly 7:30. She hadn't slept past six o'clock in years. The disruption felt physically disorienting, as if her internal chronometer had been reset by breaking into military facilities and discovering coordinated conspiracy.

Her muscles ached in places she hadn't known existed. Not from exertion, but from the dull fatigue of decisions made too close to disaster.

Her hands still remembered the cold stone floor, the weight of thermite evidence, the terror of boots approaching their hiding place.

But underneath the exhaustion was something sharper. Intellectual fury at how perfectly Shori was positioning herself.

The morning papers made her coffee taste like acid:

COUNCIL CALLS EMERGENCY SESSION ON CHIEF MINISTER'S FITNESS
Opposition Leaders Question Garda's Capacity Following Family Crisis

ASHFORD EMERGES AS STABILITY CANDIDATE
Sources Praise Minister's Steady Leadership During Transition

FISHING EXPANSION APPROVED FOR FAST-TRACK REVIEW
Northern Development Initiative Gains Momentum

Not Shori's name in the attacks, of course. Other politicians doing the dirty work while she remained above the fray, the steady hand in crisis.

The fishing expansion particularly stung. Pence's careful environmental policies, dismantled before he'd even officially resigned.

Brilliant. Absolutely brilliant and utterly vicious.

The secure phone rang with its distinctive purr.

"Progress report?" Nessa's voice carried operational efficiency and barely concealed irritation.

"Good morning to you, too," Victoria said, looking at her coffee pot, debating whether the effort would be worth it.

"Save it. Time's wasting. What have you found?"

Victoria started measuring grounds while she talked. "Shori's calendar shows remarkable prescience. Cleared schedule for Jaden's assessment day. Emergency meetings scheduled before the emergency occurred."

"Could be coincidence. Calendar management isn't conspiracy evidence. Need something concrete."

"I'm working on it." Victoria snapped, her fury transferring to her condescending partner. "Unlike some people, I understand how institutional operations function. I don't need tactical guidance from someone whose methodology emphasizes breaking laws over analytical precision."

"What you need is common sense," Nessa retorted with dangerous quiet. "Stay put. Don't play hero. Amateur hour gets people killed."

Victoria hung up with more force than necessary.

Time to demonstrate what analytical training could accomplish.

The secure phone rang again almost immediately. Victoria snatched it up, expecting Nessa's condescending follow-up.

"Ms. Colwell?" Harrison's voice carried his characteristic anxiety. "I'm terribly sorry to bother you at home, but Deputy Aide Kellworth was just here looking for you specifically. He seemed quite distressed. Mentioned something about fortress maintenance records and needing to speak with you urgently."

Victoria felt her pulse spike. "Did he say what kind of information?"

"No ma'am, just that it was sensitive and he couldn't trust normal channels. He asked when you'd be in today."

Kellworth panicking. Reaching out for help. And after Nessa's dismissive attitude about needing "concrete evidence," this could be exactly what they needed.

"Harrison, if you can locate him, tell him I'll meet him in the service tunnels beneath Treasury Building. Junction T-7. One hour. Discreet location away from potential surveillance."

"The maintenance tunnels, ma'am?"

"Just find him," she said sharply, the words flying from her mouth before good judgment could intervene. The tone shocked both her and Harrison.

"I... apologies, Harrison. Kellworth may be key to resolving a very important matter. Timing is critical."

"Will do, ma'am," Harrison replied with a click.

Victoria poured herself a fresh cup of coffee and started itemizing questions for Kellworth, ranking them by priority.

0920 | Service Tunnels, Government District

The service tunnels beneath CAD Hamilton's government district hummed with the mechanical heartbeat of a capital city: steam pipes, electrical conduits, and ventilation systems threading between buildings like arteries beneath skin. Victoria descended through the Treasury Building's maintenance access, her footsteps echoing in the concrete corridor.

She'd chosen Junction T-7 specifically. Far enough from main thoroughfares to ensure privacy, still within the secure government complex. It felt appropriately covert without being dramatic.

Victoria checked her timepiece, then positioned herself near the intersection where four tunnels converged. Overhead, utility grates allowed thin streams of morning light to cut through the underground gloom, creating pools of illumination in the mechanical darkness.

Martin Kellworth appeared exactly on schedule, emerging from the Treasury tunnel with wild-eyed panic. When he spotted her, relief flooded his features.

"Ms. Colwell, thank god." He rushed toward her. "You have to help me reach Chief Minister Garda. They're going to kill me. I know too much."

"Mr. Kellworth, please calm down," she said with authority that had resolved countless ministerial crises. "We're completely private here. Tell me systematically what you know."

"They recruited me eighteen months ago." He glanced nervously at the tunnel entrances. "Financial pressure, family medical bills. Exactly the leverage that makes people compliant."

"Who recruited you specifically?" Victoria pulled out her recording device.

"Everything was compartmentalized. But the materials I procured, the access I provided..." He pulled out a manila folder with shaking hands. "Look at this. Anonymous memos with coded instructions. Facility authorizations that bypass normal protocols."

Victoria leaned forward, studying the documents in the filtered light from above. Documentary evidence that could expose the entire network.

"I never knew they planned to hurt anyone," Kellworth continued, his voice breaking. "When that boy fell... when I understood what they'd actually used those materials for... I realized I wasn't just some corrupt administrator. I was accessory to attempted murder."

Footsteps echoed from the junction behind them.

Commander Pa emerged from the shadows with his usual military bearing. But his expression carried no surprise at finding them there. No confusion about the meeting. Just grim, professional resolve.

"Commander," Victoria said, feeling the first flutter of unease. "I wasn't expecting..."

Pa's service weapon appeared in his hand with fluid efficiency. The sharp crack of gunfire echoed through the tunnel system before Victoria could process what was happening.

Kellworth crumpled to the concrete floor, manila folder scattering papers across the maintenance corridor.

Victoria stared as Pa turned the weapon toward her. His expression carried years of friendship mixed with something approaching regret.

"I'm sorry, Victoria," he said quietly, his voice heavy with genuine pain. "You shouldn't have gotten involved in this."

"Pa, what are you doing?" Her voice barely above a whisper. "We've known each other for years. You helped tell me about Marcus. You were there when..."

"I know." His weapon hand trembled slightly. Years of friendship warring with whatever forces had brought him to this moment. "Heaven help me, I know."

Victoria saw the hesitation in his eyes and her mouth began working without conscious direction, the precision instrument that had served her through a decade of diplomatic crises deploying itself against the most personal crisis she'd ever faced.

"This is insane, Pa. You're a good man. You've served with honor for decades. Whatever they're threatening you with, whatever leverage they have, we can find another way. You don't have to..."

"SHUT UP!" Pa's voice cracked with desperate fury, echoing off concrete walls. "You have no idea what they'll do. What they've already done. My daughter, my grandchildren, if I don't follow orders, they disappear. Do you understand? They just disappear."

The weapon steadied, pointing directly at Victoria's chest. She saw Pa's finger tighten on the trigger, saw him steel himself for what came next.

The sharp crack of rifle fire echoed through the tunnel system.

Pa staggered backward, his chest blooming red. He looked down at the spreading stain with something approaching relief, then collapsed beside Kellworth's body.

Victoria looked up to see Nessa dropping through the utility grate above, landing in a controlled crouch with rifle still raised. She'd removed the grate entirely, creating a perfect shooting position overlooking the junction.

Victoria couldn't move. Couldn't speak. Could only stare at Pa's form while her mind tried to process that she'd been seconds away from execution by someone she'd considered family.

"Victoria." Nessa's voice carried command authority as she scanned the tunnels. "Are you hurt?"

Victoria opened her mouth. Nothing came out. Her legs gave way and she found herself sitting on the tunnel floor, staring at Kellworth's body and Pa's bleeding form and scattered documents.

Pa stirred. Blood frothing at his lips. Trying to speak.

Nessa knelt beside him, rifle ready.

"My family," Pa whispered. Barely audible in the mechanical hum. "Please. You have no idea what they'll do to my family when they find out I failed."

His eyes found Victoria. Something like apology flickering across his features. Then they closed.

Nessa checked his pulse. Studied his face for a long moment with an expression Victoria couldn't read. Professional calculation mixed with something that might have been recognition of a man who'd been trapped the same way she'd trapped others.

"He's alive," Nessa said. "Barely." She stood, already thinking three steps ahead. "We're going to have a chat real soon, Commander. I promise you that."

She moved to Victoria. Her voice gentler than Victoria had ever heard it.

"Victoria, look at me. Are you injured?"

Victoria's eyes focused on Nessa. She nodded quickly. Finally found her voice, though it came out as a whisper. "How did you even find me down here?"

"Really? Underground tunnels in the government district?" Nessa replied with characteristic bluntness, holstering her rifle. "Victoria, there are exactly four access points to this junction. I've been watching all of them since you left your apartment."

Heat rose in Victoria's cheeks. "You were watching me."

"Of course I was watching you. I was afraid you would do something stupid." She gestured at Kellworth's body and Pa's unconscious form and the scattered documents. "Oh look, you did something stupid."

"I thought I could handle it. I thought the tunnels would provide good... tactical advantage?"

"You mean 'concealment.' And no, they don't. Underground tunnel with limited exits isn't tactical advantage. It's a kill box."

Victoria struggled to her feet, still shaky. "I thought somewhere private and secure..."

"What's next, meeting in a cemetery at midnight?" Nessa shook her head.

Victoria looked at this woman who'd been tracking her movements, who'd positioned herself for overwatch through a utility grate, who'd dropped into a tunnel and put a round through a man's chest without hesitation.

"You know what, Nessa?" Victoria said, her voice growing stronger. "You are the most terrifying woman I have ever known."

"Terrifying?"

"You've been following me since I left my apartment. You positioned yourself above us through that grate. You dropped down here and shot Pa without hesitation. That's not just professional competence. That's absolutely terrifying."

Nessa studied her expression. Something like affection flickered before professional sharpness returned.

"Your meddling cost us a valuable witness," she said, gesturing at Kellworth's body. "He might have provided intelligence about the entire network. Now all his information dies with him."

She glanced at Pa. "This one might be more useful alive. Assuming he cooperates. Which he will, because I'm going to explain his options in terms that don't require a University of Keth education to understand."

Victoria felt the rebuke land. "I understand."

"Consider that the next time you want to play in my world, princess. I may not be there next time to scrape you off tunnel walls."

Victoria nodded.

Nessa began securing the scene, already making calls on frequencies Victoria didn't recognize. Pa would be moved. Treated. Kept alive and kept hidden until Nessa was ready for that chat she'd promised.

Victoria watched this woman who'd just saved her life while making it clear that such salvation came with expectations she was only beginning to understand.

.

PART SEVEN

THE PRICE OF SILENCE

Mid-Spring, 2183 | 1400 | Victoria's Apartment
CAD Hamilton, CA

Victoria's hands trembled slightly as she folded the morning newspaper, though whether from exhaustion or fury, she couldn't say. She hadn't slept properly in three days. Every time she closed her eyes, she saw Kellworth falling, heard the crack of Nessa's rifle, felt the cold weight of understanding what her "analytical precision" had nearly cost her.

The headlines stared back with brutal efficiency:

ASHFORD CONFIRMED AS CHIEF MINISTER
Council Votes Overwhelming Confidence in New Leadership

GARDA STEPS DOWN CITING HEALTH CONCERNS
Former Chief Minister: "Time to Focus on Family"

NEW ERA OF INSTITUTIONAL SECURITY
Enhanced Oversight Committees Receive Full Authorization

ASHFORD APPROVES NORTHERN FISHING EXPANSION
"Sustainable Development" Initiative to Boost Regional Economy

Each headline a personal defeat disguised as democratic process. The fishing expansion particularly stung. She remembered Pence's careful concerns about ecosystem stability, his warnings about species that played roles beyond their apparent significance. Now Shori was reversing years of environmental protection with the same systematic efficiency she'd applied to everything else.

Not a coup. A seamless transition that made systematic betrayal appear to be natural political evolution.

The vote hadn't even been close. Seventeen to three.

Her secure phone buzzed.

"Seen the headlines?" Nessa's voice carried operational assessment and barely concealed irritation. "Shori's winning every round."

"Not for long," Victoria replied. "I have ideas developing."

"Your ideas get people killed. Stay safe, stay smart, and for the love of all that's holy, don't try to be clever without backup."

"I don't need operational mothering from someone whose social skills apparently peaked at criminal intimidation."

Nessa's laugh carried no humor. "My 'criminal intimidation' keeps you alive, princess. Don't forget that when your educated mouth starts writing checks your survival skills can't cash."

The call ended with characteristic abruptness. Victoria checked her timepiece, her fingers lingering on the familiar bronze weight longer than usual, as if seeking comfort from its consistent reliability.

Time to face whatever came next.

✧

1400 | CAD Hamilton Medical Center
— ❖ —

Victoria walked through the medical center corridors, each step carrying the weight of knowledge she could never share and decisions that would define the rest of her life.

She found Pence in the family waiting area outside Jaden's room, and for the first time in weeks, he looked peaceful. Not the broken man she'd left after the "Vicky" moment, but someone who'd found clarity in focusing on what actually mattered. The weight of continental governance had lifted from his shoulders, leaving behind the grandfather who'd always existed beneath the political figure.

"Good afternoon, sir."

"Victoria." Pence's smile carried genuine warmth. "Perfect timing. The doctors just finished their assessment. Remarkable progress."

He gestured toward Jaden's room with obvious satisfaction. "Full sensation returning to his legs. Mobility improving daily. They're talking about adaptive training programs, ways for him to channel his analytical gifts into civilian service."

Victoria felt her chest tighten as she recognized Shori's influence in the medical coordination, the specialist consultations, the "adaptive training" that would keep Jaden close and grateful. But watching Pence's genuine happiness, she understood the cost of revelation would far exceed any benefit truth might provide.

"That's wonderful news," she managed.

"Shori's been instrumental in coordinating everything," Pence continued with obvious gratitude. "Visiting twice a week, ensuring he has access to the best specialists, even discussing scholarship opportunities. I don't know what we would have done without her support through this crisis."

Each word confirmation of systematic manipulation disguised as family devotion.

"She's been very generous with her time," Victoria said carefully.

"Like a daughter," Pence replied. The paternal pride in his voice made Victoria's knowledge feel like a weapon she could never use. "In fact, she was just here this morning, discussing internship opportunities that would allow Jaden to contribute to continental governance despite his physical limitations."

Pence studied her expression with attention that had sustained him through seven decades of political complexity. "Victoria," he said quietly, "sometimes the most important service we can provide to people we care about is protecting them from knowledge that would cause pain without enabling meaningful action."

The words landed with crystalline clarity. He was giving her permission to maintain whatever silence she deemed necessary. But underneath his careful phrasing, she caught something else. A flicker of awareness that suggested he suspected more than he was acknowledging.

"Yes, sir. Sometimes protecting those we love requires accepting burdens they shouldn't have to carry."

"Whatever truths you're carrying," Pence continued with grandfatherly concern that made her throat tighten, "just make sure they serve more than they destroy. The long game requires patience, not immediate satisfaction."

She nodded, understanding that he was providing guidance for a war he couldn't officially acknowledge but suspected she was fighting.

"Now," he said, standing with obvious anticipation, "would you like to visit with Jaden? He's been asking about you."

✿

1430 | Jaden's Room

— ❖ —

Jaden was propped up in bed, looking remarkably like the confident young man who'd approached the climbing wall weeks earlier. His color was good, his eyes clear, and his smile carried genuine pleasure at seeing her.

"Victoria! Grandfather says you've been coordinating with Minister Ashford about my recovery program. I can't thank you enough."

"Minister Ashford has been very thorough in ensuring you receive excellent care," Victoria replied with precision that maintained accuracy while concealing devastating context.

"She's amazing, isn't she?" Jaden continued with obvious admiration, though Victoria caught a brief flicker of something. Not quite doubt. Perhaps wistfulness for simpler times. "The way she's coordinated specialists, arranged adaptive training, even discussed potential roles where I could contribute despite physical limitations."

He paused, his expression growing thoughtful. "Sometimes I miss the straightforward nature of military training. Everything was so clear. Objectives, methods, success criteria. This civilian path feels more complicated."

A spark of hope at his momentary uncertainty. Beneath Shori's careful cultivation, Jaden's analytical mind was still working.

"But Minister Ashford has helped me understand that there are other ways to serve," he continued, enthusiasm returning. "The internship program she mentioned sounds promising. Working with enhanced oversight committees, learning about specialized security operations that protect constitutional government from threats that conventional oversight might miss."

Enhanced oversight committees. Specialized security operations. Shori was already recruiting Jaden for exactly the sort of systematic institutional replacement that had destroyed his original future.

"She says my cognitive assessments and pattern recognition capabilities would be particularly valuable for identifying threats that operate beyond normal procedural detection," Jaden added with growing intellectual excitement. "Constitutional government requires protection from systematic corruption that might appear legitimate on surface analysis."

The irony was so complete that Victoria had to suppress inappropriate laughter. Shori was positioning Jaden to become part of the very network that had targeted him, while convincing him he was protecting constitutional government from exactly the sort of threats she represented.

"That sounds like a wonderful opportunity to apply your analytical talents," Victoria managed.

"Grandfather seems so much happier now," Jaden observed. "I think stepping away from political pressures has allowed him to focus on what really matters. *We focus on those living,* as he always says."

"He's a remarkable man," Victoria agreed with genuine affection.

What she didn't say was that this peace required her continued silence about systematic betrayal. That protecting Pence's happiness meant watching Jaden being recruited by the very person who'd destroyed his original dreams while believing she was helping him build new ones.

What she didn't say was that her analytical capabilities had revealed conspiracy requiring response through methods that constitutional government couldn't officially acknowledge, and which might take decades to implement.

Her secure phone buzzed discreetly. A message from Shori's office: "Looking forward to coordinating Jaden's internship opportunities. Your administrative expertise will be invaluable for ensuring seamless integration with enhanced oversight operations."

Victoria looked at Jaden's eager face. At Pence's peaceful satisfaction visible through the doorway. And made her choice.

✧

1500 | Departure
— ❖ —

Pence walked her to the medical center entrance with the sort of grandfatherly attention that reminded her why she'd devoted eight years of her life to serving his vision of constitutional government.

"Victoria," he said quietly as they reached the doors, "I want you to know that whatever path you choose going forward, you have my complete trust and support. The work you've done, the loyalty you've shown, the wisdom you've developed. All of it will serve you well in whatever comes next."

Victoria felt tears threaten. "Thank you, sir. For everything you've taught me about service, about sacrifice, about focusing on what truly matters."

Pence nodded, his eyes holding the quiet pride of a mentor who'd watched his student grow beyond what he could have imagined.

"Remember," he said with final wisdom that felt like both blessing and warning, "the most important victories are often the ones nobody sees. Patience, precision, and persistence. Those are the tools that build lasting change rather than temporary satisfaction."

Victoria stepped into the afternoon light. The medical center doors closed behind her with the quiet efficiency of institutional architecture serving its designed purpose.

She checked her timepiece. Half past three. The afternoon train to Hamilton departed in forty-seven minutes, which left adequate time to walk to the station at a pace that didn't suggest either urgency or retreat.

Marcus had died serving something larger than himself. Pence had built a career protecting principles that outlasted the people who held them. Jaden had climbed a wall because that was what Garda men did.

And Shori Ashford had learned, over decades of careful work, that the most effective way to destroy an institution was to become it.

Victoria adjusted her briefcase. Straightened her collar. Small gestures of order applied to a world that had become profoundly disordered.

She had been an aide. A scheduler. A manager of grain disputes and infrastructure proposals and the enthusiastic incompetence that passed for frontier governance.

She was something else now. She didn't have a word for it yet. But the word would come, in time, the way the right policy language always came when you understood the problem clearly enough.

Victoria walked toward the station with her usual precise stride. Forty-seven minutes. More than sufficient.

She had work to do.

NESSA CODA

THE NETWORK FORMS

Late Spring, 2183 | Hamilton Central Library
CAD Hamilton, CA

—— ❖ ——

I arrived at the library fifteen minutes early. Two exits. One security guard reading a newspaper. A maintenance corridor behind the reference desk that probably connected to the building next door. Recent events had sharpened everything, especially when dealing with an amateur partner whose talent for walking into mortal danger exceeded even my expectations.

Victoria Colwell approached our table with that same precise timing that marked her background, though something fundamental had shifted in her bearing since our last confrontation. The protective shell was still there, but it felt different now. Less brittle. More purposeful. Like someone who'd learned exactly how close intellectual pride could come to getting her killed.

She settled into her chair, consulting her timepiece openly. A gesture I'd been watching for weeks. My curiosity was getting the better of me.

"What time do you have?" I asked.

Victoria consulted her timepiece with that same habitual precision I'd observed throughout our partnership. "Five forty-seven, precisely."

I studied her expression, then glanced at the library clock showing nearly five forty-seven in the evening. "Amazing. Do you even realize you do that anymore?"

"Whatever do you mean?" Victoria looked genuinely puzzled.

"The timepiece. I first noticed the hands were frozen when we met. Thought it was odd, but figured you'd get it repaired. Then again after the shooting, you checked it the same way, with that same confidence." I leaned forward. "The hands haven't moved once, Victoria."

Victoria's expression shifted, surprise giving way to something approaching fond recognition. She smiled softly and rubbed the timepiece's surface with unmistakable affection.

"You are perhaps the first to notice, outside Pence of course. But he lets me play my little game, fascinated by how I manage to keep precise time despite..." She paused, her voice growing quieter. "Truth is, Ms. Kaine, this timepiece is stuck. Frozen at the moment my world changed, and I have yet to move on."

She held the mechanism up to catch the library's warm light, her thumb tracing the crystal face with reverence.

"Marcus Holt was my betrothed. Well, that's perhaps presumptuous. He never actually proposed, but I learned he'd inquired about a ring and set aside a special date I wish I could know." Her voice carried weight that made our strategic planning feel suddenly secondary to something far more personal.

"Marcus died trying to help Pence's daughter and son-in-law survive a bridge collapse over Sarin Bay. Ninety passengers plunged to their deaths in those cold waters. Marcus was found outside the wreckage, pulling Penny through an open window. Something had held her back, and he drowned saving her instead of saving himself."

Underneath her analytical precision, I caught the tremor of grief that time hadn't healed.

"Word didn't reach me for three days. A cruel joke, not being aware that your life has fundamentally changed for three whole days. Pence and Commander Pa broke the news together." Her voice softened with memory. "'Vicky, you should sit down. What I'm about to tell you is not pleasant.' I can still hear that gentleness in his voice. Here was a man whose daughter had just died, concerned about my feelings."

She looked up from the timepiece, meeting my eyes directly. "'We remember those who lived, but we focus on those still alive,' he said. What a pompous thing to say... and I love him all the more for it."

Victoria's smile carried both pain and genuine affection. "That moment was at two-seventeen in the afternoon. This is all I have of him, Ms. Kaine. And someday, perhaps, I will see him again."

"Five years," I said quietly.

"Five years, two months, and six days," Victoria corrected with characteristic precision. "Not that I'm counting."

✿

"Grateful?" The word surprised me.

"You saved my life the other night, Vanessa. But more than that..." She paused, searching for words. "You showed me I could actually do something. For eight years, I've watched terrible things happen and filed reports about them. You showed me some rules aren't worth following."

The rawness caught me off guard. This wasn't diplomatic courtesy.

"You want to know something?" I said. "You had more guts going after Shori than I've had in years."

Victoria actually snorted. An extraordinary sound from someone whose vocal range typically peaked at dry observation. "Guts? I nearly got myself killed being an idiot."

"Stupid, yeah. But brave stupid." Something loosened in my chest that I hadn't known was tight. "I've been playing it safe for years, telling myself I was protecting the system. Truth is, I was protecting myself."

"Pence called for you specifically," Victoria said quietly. "He doesn't trust easily anymore."

"He called for me because I've screwed things up before." The admission came out rougher than I intended. "I've been on the wrong side too many times, Victoria. I'm tired of it."

She studied me. The sharp look was still there, but it had changed. She was seeing me instead of analyzing me. The difference was small but I felt it.

"We're both looking for a chance to fix things, aren't we?" she said.

"Something like that."

She opened her notebook. Victoria Colwell opening a notebook was the equivalent of a general unfurling a map. It meant the conversation was about to acquire structure.

"I've been mapping what Shori's actually building," she said. Charts. Organizational diagrams. More sophisticated than I'd expected from someone who'd been managing grain shipments two weeks ago. "It's not political maneuvering. She's replacing the entire system. Patient, methodical, completely ruthless."

"And we're years behind her."

"Yes." Victoria's precision was back, but it sat differently now. Harder. "We need more than sneaking around and shooting people. We need institutional knowledge and operational capability working together."

"You want to civilize me," I said.

"I want us to fight her on equal ground." Her smile was sharp enough to cut with. "The question is whether you're willing to try."

I found myself considering it. Not tactically. As something that might matter.

"Constitutional government protected by unconstitutional methods," she said. "We have time. She thinks she's already won."

She checked her timepiece. The gesture carried new meaning now that I understood what those frozen hands held.

"This is going to take years," she said.

"The important things usually do."

◈

As we reached the library entrance, I stopped. "Victoria. For what it's worth, I'm glad you're still here. After Marcus, after everything."

Her expression softened, hand moving unconsciously to her timepiece. "Thank you. That means more than you know."

She looked out at the Hamilton streets. "Marcus died serving something larger than himself. Maybe this is how I honor that."

We stepped into the evening together.

I watched Victoria walk down Hamilton's main street. That precise stride. Unchanged despite everything. Most people crack after what she'd been through. She walked straighter.

I found a bench in the park across from the library and sat with Pence's letter, reading it again in the lamplight:

Agent Kaine — Victoria doesn't know what she's walking into, but I suspect you do. Someone orchestrated my grandson's attack with surgical precision. I have my suspicions about who, but can't prove anything without endangering my family further. Protect her. Help her find the truth. When the time comes for justice, it must be complete and quiet. Some wars require patience. We must focus on those still living. — P.G.

That old man. He'd known what Victoria would do. Known how reckless she'd be. Known exactly why I'd need to keep her alive despite herself.

I folded the letter and sat with the weight of it. Anne, out there somewhere, carrying the damage I'd done to her. Regal, hunting through territories I'd aimed him at and walked away from. Victoria, walking into a war I'd been avoiding for years.

Three people I'd touched. Three people changed by the touching. The pattern wasn't lost on me.

But Victoria was different. I hadn't found her broken. I'd found her furious. And fury, properly directed, was something I'd learned to respect.

The memory hit without warning. Fort Delvaine. Twenty-two years ago. The same climbing wall. The same ancient stones. I'd been younger, faster, just as determined. Shori had been waiting at the top when I finished, her face bright with pride.

"You made it," she'd said, pulling me up onto the platform. "I knew you would."

We'd been so different then.

"Cadet Shori Ashford," I said to the empty park. The smile that came with the memory faded as the eager young woman transformed into Chief Minister Ashford. Something settled over me that was older than strategy and heavier than operational planning.

"In time," I whispered. "One of us will fall."

ABOUT THE AUTHOR

JT Baldwin spent thirty years carrying the world of Blood & Steel before he ever wrote it down. The first sketches lived in notebooks shared with his twin brother — game designs, comic characters, half-built mythologies that never quite let him go. They matured in silence through a career that took him from military service to long-haul trucking across the country, the kind of work that leaves a person alone with their thoughts for ten hours at a time. The characters traveled with him.

The Blood & Steel saga foundation is built on three interlocking series: the Ironforged novels, beginning with *Wilted Crowns*; *The Palisade Journals*, a five-novella collection charting the decades of conspiracy and resistance that shape everything to come; and *Forged in Blood & Steel*, an ongoing collection of short stories from the world. He believes the best stories leave readers with something worth thinking about long after the last page — and that the second read should be richer than the first.

He lives in southeastern Minnesota with his wife, where the world keeps growing and the winters are too damn cold and long.

www.ingramcontent.com/pod-product-compliance
Lightning Source LLC
Chambersburg PA
CBHW022047170626
46808CB00003B/1389